DISCOVERY of GLOW

DISCOVERY of GLOW

Written by

Jennifer Jazwierska

&

Candice Bataille Popiel

Illustration & Design

Thom Buchanan

Jill Haller

Glowmundo Creations LLC

Discovery of Glow
By
Jennifer Jazwierska and Candice Bataille Popiel
Book I of the Glowmundo Series

Text copyright © 2008 by Glowmundo Creations LLC
Illustration copyright © 2008 by Glowmundo Creations LLC

Illustrated & Designed by Thom Buchanan & Jill Haller

Published in 2008 by Glowmundo Creations, LLC
Arvada, Colorado
© 2008 Glowmundo Creations LLC

Printed in China by WorkflowOne

For information contact:
www.glowmundo.com

Cover Illustration & Design by Thom Buchanan & Jill Haller

ISBN 13-digit: 978-0-9814930-0-8
Library of Congress Control Number: 2008900488

Cast of Characters

Lumina Osity
"Leaping Light Beams!"

Known as Little Miss Oxford, since she has a fact for every purpose

Astronomy Connoisseur

Hats are her signature, socks are her passion

Blinking buddies are her firefly pets, the cocuyos

Doodles in constellations

Peeks at the world through experimentation

Burst *"Slam Dunk"*

Plays most sports

Fastest kid on the track team

Set town record in 2005 for longest time hanging upside-down

Biggest tester-outer of Lumina's inventions

Grand Champion of never sitting still

Shantanu *"Relax, Dude"*

Originally from India

De Om Jammin dude

Speaks cocuyo which he learned from ancient mentors

Will win any smile-a-thon

His motto is "go with the flow"

Magnitude *"Hey, Stargazer"*

Has a magnitude of attitude

Never seen without her twin friends

She seems to have a permanent stuck-on frown

Won the best grumbler award

Happy seems far from her mind

Orion   "Let's chart this plan"

Lumina's inventor brother

Chief Family Engineer (CFE)

Designer of the award winning Leaf Terminator

Always up to his elbows in blueprints

His pockets are always filled with gadgets: alligator clips, bolts, pliers and colored wires

Ivy "I'll stage it for ya"

Lumina's next door neighbor

Leader of the Theater Club

Set and costume designer

Groovy funk dresser

Omnia "Hey, Girlfriend"

Lumina's classmate

Spends free time outdoors and with horses

Experiments with organic food combinations

Chief Environmentalist

Mr. Semple "Okay, geniuses"

Teacher of Classroom Number Eight

Creator of the best lessons in the school

Teaches from Center Stage

His graduate dissertation was entitled "The Power of the Mind"

Cast of Pets

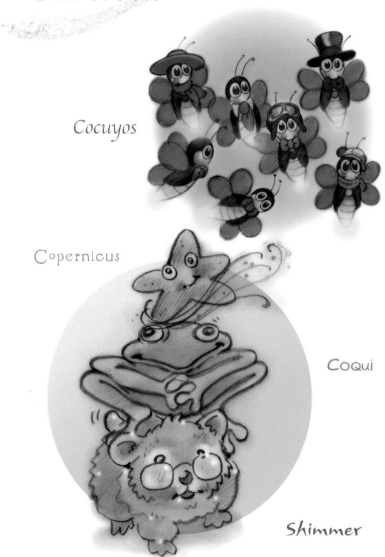

Cocuyos

Copernicus

Coqui

Shimmer

The Beginning

I knew I was dreaming. As I dodged the glowing balls that whizzed by me, I moved like a cat, jumping two times my own height. My friends and I were playing a glowing dodgeball game. Each ball we created had a different purpose. My own thought instantly created a purple tickle ball, my specialty. Burst, my friend, dove to narrowly escape a turquoise ball. He could not see me, so I made my move. I watched as my purple specialty hit his leg and began to tickle his foot right inside his shoe. Burst wiggled, giggled and yelled as he tried to pry off his shoe. "Woohoo," I yelled with my hands in the air. Then out of the corner of my eye, I saw it right before it happened. A green ball was heading right for my stomach. "No! Not the Mind Muck ball." But it was too late. It hit me and the green expanded in every direction, to my legs, arms and brain. A fog crept into my head. I couldn't think straight. I knew I needed to move fast, because I didn't want to get lost in the fog. But slow was the only speed my brain was doing. As I began to panic, I suddenly heard a huge voice boom inside my head. It said:

Find your glow--Then you will know exactly where to go.

I *shifted* my thoughts, and I quickly started to feel better.

That's when I woke up as something was shaking my shoulders. Yikes! Two full-moon-shaped eyes wide open behind giant pink sunglasses were two inches from my nose! I screamed and pushed the eyes away.

Sitting up in bed, I realized that the eyes belonged to my older brother, Orion, who was wearing my Flaming Star Shades. Whew! Looking around, I relaxed. I was still in my Celestial Science Observatory, otherwise known as my bedroom. The CS Observatory is at the top of our awesome Light House. My mom, an architect, redesigned and remodeled this wonderful old place on the edge of Iridescent Village. It is a one-of-a-kind spectacular creation with a way-cool set of 68 winding steps that take me up to my room. This Light House, as you might imagine, sits on a cliff overlooking the sea. It is filled with many nooks and crannies that my brother and I have been famous for turning into hideaways.

What's up with the shine?" Ori asked. "You look like you just swallowed a year's supply of mom's moonbeam cakes," he said, squinting at me.

"Ori, thanks for waking me up. Now I remember that *you* are just the person I need to see. I need you to draft the plans for something," I said.

I jumped out of bed. My foot landed on a rocket-propelled wheelie shoe shooting me forward, knocking the door open. My hamster,

"Shimmer", started shaking in shock. At the exact same time, I lost my balance and stumbled, accidentally knocking my rock collection into a moonflower pot, which tipped over into the hamster cage. Shimmer, covered in rocks and dirt, happily escaped with lightning speed to hide under my table, the Experimentation Station.

"Shimmer," I gasped, running after him. "I didn't mean to give you a meteor shower so early in the morning." Shimmer looked up at me with terrified eyes.

Ori, who was watching all of the action from under my Cosmic Viewer Telescope Model Number 5580, stood up to feed "Copernicus", my pet starfish. I started searching for my Light Journal. Ori shaded his eyes and pretended to faint as I walked by.

"Lums, you're so bright I have to shield my eyes!" Ori teased.

I looked at Ori. He was rolling his eyes. "I am still waiting," he said, "What's with the new look?" Ori asked.

"OK." I stopped what I was doing and turned to face him. "It's a good thing it's Saturday. Sit. Open your ears, and shade your eyes. Now read this," I said.

I handed him my Light Journal, and he began to read. (My Light Journal is the notebook where I write down all the super-stellar stuff that happens, as well as the not-so-super-stellar stuff. I carry it with me everywhere for when something cool happens).

Please
ask Permission
before reading
this!

If
found
Please
return to
3303 South
Blinking Lane

This is my
LIGHT
JOURNAL

By,

Lumina

Osity

Lumina
Osity

Private!

Glow

Chapter One

I was in my CS Observatory one night getting ready to catch some z's.

I was dressed in my favorite twinkling jammies. I love it that they glow in the dark and have dancing fireflies all over them. Sometimes I have trouble sleeping because my pet *cocuyos* start following me around trying to make friends with the fireflies on my jammies. Instantly these stellar critters flew over and gathered around me.

Cocuyos means "fireflies" in Spanish. My dad and his family speak Spanish.

"Shoo flies don't bother me, time for me to get some z's," I sang, shooing them in the direction of their lantern. I picked up my butterfly net and carefully guided them into their nightlight. Their nightlight is a mini lantern that glows when they are inside. When I closed the little hinged door, the nightlight lit up with their yellow-gold light, making patterns on the walls of my room.

Phew, now I could relax!

Next, I did my regular bedtime rotation. First, I checked the water levels in Copernicus' tank. Wouldn't want him to experience low tide before morning. Then I pulled down the shades in Shimmer's cage.

"Sweet moonbeams, Shimmy," I whispered.

Finally, I climbed the three steps to my telescope and peered out into the night sky. Each night I search for a special constellation of the day. That night it was Taurus, the bull. I was standing there looking up at this heavenly sight when my mom called to me.

"Lumina, äskling," said my Swedish mom, "You need to go to sleep now, it is past your bedtime," she called from the doorway. "God natt." she whispered as she blew me a kiss. Then she switched off the light and disappeared down the stairs.

My glow-in-the-dark constellations showed up on the walls to say goodnight.

"G'night, Mamma," I called softly, listening to her footsteps fade as she went down the staircase.

Following the star paths along the walls, I

climbed into bed. It was suddenly very quiet. I tried to go to sleep, but big, scary shadows leaped wherever I looked. One shadow looked like my Aunt Lightey wearing rollers! Another form was a tall, skinny blob with hundreds of creepy fingers. I was feeling all wiggly and scared so I pulled the covers up to my nose.

Oooh, I was full of Mind Muck. Tonight it was oozing around and around, making it impossible for me to sleep. Where could this have come from? This stuff was freaking me out. Earlier, I had watched a few episodes of "Bratty Boy, the Scare Wizard". Maybe that had stirred it up. I've noticed that watching TV can change my mood.

Mind Muck is my way of saying many yucky thoughts

The more I tried to go to sleep, the more it seemed like my thoughts were spinning like Shimmer on his wheel. Those thoughts ran faster, circling around and around. I tried burrowing deeper under the blankets. I squished into a space under my pillow. But that Mind Muck stuck, hanging in my mind like gooey glue. I was sweating like a Venus desert in July. I knew I had to do something.

So, like a shooting star I jumped up, pushed back the covers, and reached over the craft stuff on my nightstand to snap on my light. Oops, I accidentally knocked over a whole bottle of glitter from my school art project. It spread lightning-quick all over the floor. Instantly, my bedspread and I were covered by a huge wave of sparkle.

"Shooting stars!" I muttered. Now I was scared **and** sparkly.

Starhopper

Feeling skittery and jumpy, I knew I had to move as quickly as possible in order to clean up the mess and get back to the comfort zone of my blanket. I stumbled out of bed to clean, and I noticed moonbeams floating through my window like butterflies of light. A swarm of *cocuyos* was riding on the moonbeams. ***Hey, guys are we having a party?*** I thought to myself. Then, I looked at my hands and saw they were all sparkly from the glitter. They looked a little like glimmering stars as I twirled them around. Wow, they looked spectacular! I could wave and dance them through the moonbeams and create a laser show in my room. So I began to imagine-,-no, I began to *Mind Travel.*

Mind Travel is what I call a journey in my imagination.

21

I looked up through the observatory skylights. Shooting stars filled the sky. They seemed to fall right into my bedroom. I caught one of the stars and hopped on. I was a starhopper! I held on, and the shooting star lifted me across the galaxies. I twirled around watching the crab, bubble, dumbbell, and crescent nebulas pass by. I blasted out of the Milky Way. Each galaxy I passed seemed bigger than the one before. It was awesome! My heart did a happy flip. I clung to the shooting star. It was so silent out there I could hear my heartbeat in my ears. I saw the pinwheel and sombrero galaxies. My glittering hands seemed to glow.

Suddenly there were cocuyos everywhere. I wondered again what they were up to. Then, -THUNK!- my attention landed me hard on the floor. Oops. The moment I had that worry thought, I was blasted back to my bedroom.

I sat down in the pile of glitter and shook my head, waving *cocuyos* aside. My stomach was filled with bubbling, fizzy-soda energy. My **Mind Traveling** had taken me on a roller coaster ride. I felt good. I wasn't scared anymore. The Mind Muck had oozed itself out of me. Wow! What had just happened?

My imagination, that's what had happened. Toss me a star map. What do ya' know? A little trip in my imagination, and I went from a space of Mind Muck to a space of intergalactic fun. But for now, my central combustion chamber was running on empty. Translation: I was beginning to feel *very sleepy*. Time to clean up the mess and get some sleep.

As I crawled around to collect the extra glitter dust from the floor, I saw my reflection in the mirror that was leaning against the wall. Leaping Light beams! I shrieked and fell over backwards, scattering the glitter once again. I was glowing! Wow, I looked as good on the

outside as I felt on the inside!   I snuck another
peek. A glow cloud spread out around me like a
brilliant supernova.

And, that's when I took a note, or rather, a note about glow:

Mind Muck + Thinking More Mind Muck = Feeling Yucky + Glowless

Mind Travel = Feeling _Stellar_ + _Glowful_

Finally, I cleaned up the mess, and, with a big sigh, I climbed in bed. Drifting off to sleep, I felt like I was cradled in the curve at the base of the moon. *Mmmmmmm.*

Glow Thoughts!

Chapter Three

I woke up to the sound of "Rocket", my trusty alarm clock. My brother and I designed Rocket to take off and fly around the room when we don't respond to the first wake up call. I listened to his jingle, "Blast off!" he sang. "Time to wake up. Don't roll over and go back to sleep. Come on now, one foot out of bed, now the other one. Have a great day, and don't forget to wind the clock." I jetted out of bed and turned him off before he launched. I dashed to school in record time, not only because of my rocket-propelled wheelie shoes, but also because I felt so stellar-sweet that morning. I was on top of my universe. I'd discovered something glow-rific last night and couldn't wait to find out more about it. Later that morning, I was on the playground during recess eating some of my mom's heavenly star clusters. (Star clusters are my mom's version of protein bars. My mom is a food artist.) That's when I saw my classmate Wanda walking toward me. Every footstep meant business, and her nose was high in the air. Wanda would pick on anyone who crossed her path. She was also known around town as "Magnitude" because of her giant attitude.

Whenever I saw Magnitude, I sensed a gray, rolling thick thunderhead cloud around her, like she was about to start thundering. Her friends, who are look-alike twins, were always with her like two snarling watchdogs. We used to hang out, but this year it seemed like we were on different planets because her storm cloud had gotten so thick. I could tell by her glare that today was going to be trouble.

She and the twins all glared at me, and I soon found myself bombarded by solar flares. Flying *saucers!* I got nervous and quickly glanced around to locate a hiding place, silently wishing for a black hole. Trying to look busy, I started to rummage through my "Voyager Pac," which is what I call my backpack.

"Lumina, what *are* you doing?" Magnitude jeered, "You are *such* a star gazer."

I used all of my power to ignore her. I turned my back to her, and imagined that they were all floating out into space. When I heard nothing, I glanced over my shoulder and caught Magnitude and her friends looking me up and down, giving me a once-over.

"Don't socks even match in that stupid observation station of yours?" She scoffed. "It must be too spacey out there for all of your socks to find one another." The twins snickered and kept on glaring.

Her words hit me like darts. I looked down

at my socks and felt **space rocks** gather in my
stomach as I realized that I wore one yellow

stardust sock and one blue comet sock. *Oh, this
stinks, I thought. I'd done it again. When am
I gonna get a clue and stay on planet Earth?*
I felt my glow dim as my sadness crept in, and I

started to look around to see if anyone else had noticed.

The twins started to make announcements in sing-song stereo. "Socks from another galaxy. Look at Lumina Osity. No two alike. Always weird and strange. Text Lumina for more information."

I went into shock. Gee, those twins have amplified voice boxes or something. My cell phone started buzzing immediately, and I saw people stop to stare.

Magnitude and the twins started laughing as I scrambled inside my Voyager Pac to find my phone. As she marched off, she bumped my pack, spilling all of its contents to the ground.

The smoldering, steaming impact of her words made my cheeks blush hot, as I bent down to pick up my stuff. *YEEEOOOUUUGGGGGHHHH!!!!!!!!!* I thought to myself, *they. . . will. . . be. . . sorry.* I sat down hard, feeling rejected and bummed. I wished I could transform into a giant bucket of mud and dump myself right on top of their big heads. That would be a perfect fashion statement for them. I sighed thinking it wasn't worth the trouble. Suddenly, I felt alone, like I was standing in a crater on Mars. Dust devils of sadness and anger blew in stinging my eyes. I felt tears forming.

As I put away my **Reflective Detective**, (also known as my mirror), I gasped at my reflection. *Where was my glow?* It was stuck to my head like a very bad swimming cap. *E e w w, how i c k y.*

How could I have let them walk all over me again? There they go, marching off, carrying my power with them.

Just then I thought I saw a *Cocuyo* do a fly-by. But looking around I saw that I was still alone. Touching my head, I caught a glimpse of some glitter on my hands. Gazing at the glitter, I had a sparkling positive thought. No wait, it was a glow thought because it made me feel better. Glow Thoughts. Hmm, that needed a little exploration; I pulled out my Light Journal and took another note of glow. No, wait again, a Glow Note.

Mind Muck + Thinking More Mind Muck = Feeling Yucky + Glowless

Thinking Positive Thoughts, Glow Thoughts = Feeling Stellar + Glowful

Lucky stars! How about a little experimentation? *Cocuyos* surprised me by swarming out of nowhere. They were blinking like crazy.

"Hey look, guys, can't you see that I'm a little busy? Catch ya' later," I said, waving them away.

Next, I searched through the jumble at my feet to find a test tube. What if I made a mixture of GlowThoughts? What would happen? I wonder what would happen if I mixed **Mind Travel** with GlowThoughts?

Could I **amplify** my glow again?

Someone to Hang With

It was time to *shift it*. What did I need? I needed some Glow Thoughts. What Glow Thoughts? So, I took a deep breath and asked myself a question. *Right now, what would* **amplify** *my glow?* The answer that popped into my mind at the speed of light was this: *Someone to hang with!*

So I began to whisper the Glow Thought quietly to myself. I held my test tube in my hand, and, with my other hand, I stuffed in many Glow Thoughts. Then, I sprinkled in even some more Glow Thoughts.

I find someone to hang with right now.
I find someone to hang with right now.
I find someone to hang with right now.

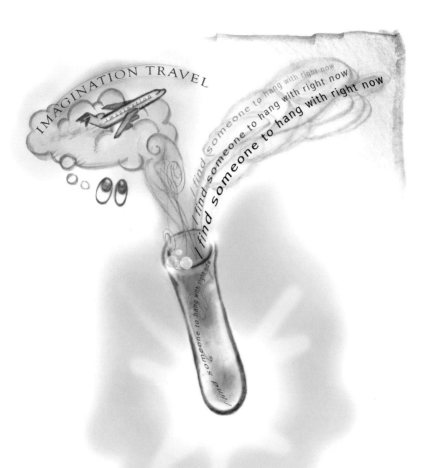

The tube began to bubble, shake, and glow!
My eyes opened wide as a glowing mixture of
bubbles began to fizz and run down my arm. As
the fizz dripped, it seemed as if the playground
was transforming into a friendly oasis of water

and green plants and trees. All of a sudden, I saw there had been kids all around me the whole time. Even when I had been hanging out with my own sadness, I was not alone. The Glow Thoughts were lifting my sadness, and now I saw kids popping up like flowers. They were even swinging on vines from the monkey bars. Whew, I began to feel the glow again.

In that exact instant, my friend, Burst,  jetted by me and began pulling me along! Burst is the fastest kid in school and plays every sport. He's particularly stellar at ice hockey and track. Around the school, he is considered the typical jock, but I know there's much more to him than that. For one thing, he's totally into learning tons of new stuff.

"Lumina, let's go. We've been waiting for you *forever* over on the monkey bars. Where have you been? Can I have some of your star clusters?" he asked all in one breath.

"Of course, Stuart T. Turnsey," I said. (That's his real name, and I only use it when I really want to get his attention). I handed him the bag.

"Hey, cut out that Stuart stuff. Lums, let's go," he said.

Then he stopped and squinted at me. He blinked a few times before he shrugged and took off running, signaling for me to follow. I smiled. The glow had returned.

Glowing Through the Village

After school that day I walked home along the main street of *Iridescent Village*. My ancestors founded the Village. I come from a long line of astronomers, you know, people who study stars and space. They built this village for the International Planetary Science Laboratory. It is now home to many scientists and astronomers who do important research here. My Venezuelan dad works in the lab as an astrophysicist.

I stopped to window shop at *Mrs. Littman's Star Sunglasses Store*. She was having a sale. The sign read: *"Gemini Deal: Two Pairs for the Price of One."* I peeked through the window and saw my favorite styles on display: Caseopia Green and **Black Scorpio**. I was instantly inspired to put on my Flaming Star shades. That's when I realized that everyone I passed was putting on their shades too.

Whoa, I really was glowing! Then I caught my reflection in the window. Gloooooowwwwwwing! What a supernova day! I felt like I had just been notified that the next newly discovered planet had been named after me. Glow **must happen when I** shift mind muck **into** Glow Thoughts. Whew, shift was tough. But, did this mean that I could glow more no matter what?

"Hey Lums, wait up!" Burst called, making me jump.

Burst ran full-blast toward me. He has sooo much energy. He's like a comet, you see. So I came up with that nickname when we were just little starlings. He never sits still. He caught up with me in only 2.2 milliseconds. We started half-walking, half-jogging down the street. We spotted Magnitude and her friends up ahead. They were hanging out at the Milky Way Ice Cream Shoppe.

"Hey, time out," Burst whispered to me. "Do

you want me to clobber that Magnitude girl? I'd say three strikes, and she's out for teasing you at recess."

"Thanks for the offer, but I'm feeling stellar now," I said.

"Are you sure?" Burst asked, studying me a little closer. "Hey, you don't look normal. You're kind of shining or something. And hey, what's that on your hands?"

"Burst, I am more than OK. I am glowing! This stuff is glitter. I have just discovered something really, really gigantic."

Burst's eyes opened wide for a second. He cleared his throat. "Lums . . . is this going to be like the time you tried to launch rockets off my roof? My parents weren't very happy about that."

"Nope, this is even better," I said.

"What is it?" Burst asked excitedly.

"Imagine this. I've discovered ways to glow. I think I've found out that you can feel good inside even when stuff on the outside doesn't seem to be going right," I said.

Burst was looking at me like I was an alien.

"Lumina, I think maybe you ate a few too many star clusters for lunch or something. You're not making sense," he said.

I studied my friend. His face was sort of scrunched up, and his eyes were glazed. I'd lost him.

"OK, Burst, why don't you jet by my house later, and we'll try an experiment."

"Yeah," he said, doing an imaginary SLaM dUNK over my head. He always did that when he thought something was cool.

"Hey, Lums," he called, "See ya' later. Don't blind anybody on your way home!"

As I turned around, I practically skipped into Magnitude and her friends and I stopped short. They glared. I stared. Suddenly, I smiled at them and kept right on going.

Terminonster

I stood in front of my garage and ducked. An alligator clip whizzed over my head at the speed of light. I could hear crashes and bangs. It looked like a tornado had touched down inside my garage! I watched a spiral of connectors, fuses, bolts, pliers, and colored wires by the dozen flying in all directions. What in the world!

As I cautiously entered the garage, I had to dodge a flying straight edge. I came face to face with my growling brother, Orion, the family engineer. I did a double take, stopping with precision force. Was he growling? He was furious, with angry words rolling from his mouth like a tsunami.

A leaf terminator is a leaf eater in the form of a model robot. (Orion invented this contraption to take over his job of raking and decomposing the leaves from our monstrous yard.)

"Hey, Lumina Osity, what did you do to my leaf terminator?" He

43

yelled.

"You *are* a total star gazer. I got the text at school," he said.

I ran into the garage and stopped short.

There was a gruesome scene of Ori's leaf terminator with pieces of my bike sticking out of its jaws. A wheel from my bike lay spinning on its side making a grotesque whining sound. Apparently my bike hadn't been put away securely, and it crashed. The Leaf Terminator must have been hungry.

"You've turned my Terminator into a metalarian. He won't ever be interested in the soft squishy leaves now that he's tasted bike parts," Ori complained.

"Well, duh, not like he gets a steady diet when you don't do your chores," I shot back.

"It's not what I do or don't do. Maybe if you spent more time on planet Earth, you would be able to see that there's other people's stuff around you. I wouldn't be surprised if you actually wake up on the moon someday," Orion said.

I could feel some of my glow shrinking rapidly.

"Hey, Ori, I am sorry. I guess my bike fell,

and your Terminonster ate it," I apologized, staring at the floor. "I could complain a little too. Just look at the remains!"

Then his words really started to flash lightning and thunder. I felt anger begin to boil deep inside me. So frustrating!!!! I wanted to flash back at him and stuff my apology in his ear. But instead I ran into the house, down the hall and into the bathroom with a whole flock of *cocuyos* leading the way. I slammed the door behind me. *I WAS REALLY MAD!!!*

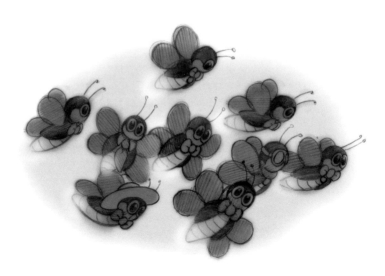

Flush it Out

I stood there and felt the clouds gathering in my mind. I felt a storm was building in my head. Things were about to get worse. This was hard work, because I was so angry. How was I going to *shift* that? The *cocuyos* were blinking like crazy flies.

"Not now guys!" I shouted, "Enough already. Bug off!"

My heart was pounding a hundred miles per hour and my face was getting redder. *OK, get a grip,* I thought. So, I grabbed the edge of the sink, took a deep breath, and started to think. Wait a minute-,-thinking got me into this. What could I do to un-think my way out? Just then I noticed a *cocuyo* buzzing around in the corner of the mirror. He buzzed and blinked and buzzed and blinked. I tried to shoo him away, but he did a dive and hit my hand, and my hand hit the faucet and turned it on. Water splashed in every direction, and I struggled to turn it off. While I was wrestling the faucet, a band of *cocuyos* landed on the handle of the toilet and flushed it! *Great, now I was locked in the bathroom with a bunch of bugs gone wild.*

Watching the water go down the drain the thought came to me. *Flush it out!* A Glow Thought!

"*Flush* **what** out?" I asked myself. Oh, I needed to *flush* this storm of Mind Muck out of my brain. That's it. What if I flushed the Mind Muck out by repeating Glow Thoughts? Would the Glow Thoughts be powerful enough?

I pulled a couple of test tubes out of Voyager Pac. I began by thinking up all of the Mind Muck, which was all the reasons I was angry with Ori. I collected it all in the first test tube. What a yucky mess! It turned an ugly shade of muddy gray and began to thunder. I jumped back to avoid some little lightning bolts that began to shoot out of

the top. The test tube was jumping like molten rocks on Venus. I quickly grabbed a cork, plugged up the tube and put it aside. Next, I created a sort of rhyme of Glow Thoughts that went something like this:

Angry words don't stay in me.
I flush them down the drain.
Angry words don't fall on me.
I don't like that kind of rain.

I repeated the rhyme over and over again and put this into the second test tube. I was beginning to feel better already and starting to get back on track. A little glow was starting to creep in. The test tube immediately started forming brilliant sparkly crystals inside. This tube felt very calm and happy, like a moonlit night. I wished I could have crawled right inside of it.

Next, I held the Glow Thoughts test tube and began to pour it into the Mind Muck test tube. The Mind Muck seemed to eat the Glow Thoughts! Quickly, I began to repeat the Glow Thoughts rhyme over and over, faster and faster. I felt the test tube shake in my hands. I watched as the crystals inside started to branch out in all directions. Soon, they formed a rainbow of colored lights that began to spill outside of the test tube. Suddenly all of the Mind Muck had disappeared. I breathed a sigh of relief. I was feeling stellar once again!!

I looked in the mirror and saw the glow shining around my head. My glow had been **amplified** while doing the experiment. I felt like I was floating without gravity! I sat down to record these new findings in my Light Journal.

Angry words don't stay in me.
I flush them down the drain.
Angry words don't fall on me.
I don't like that kind of rain.

Glow Note:

Flush It Out + Repetition of Glow Thoughts =
Glow Amplified is Glowful, Even Bigger.

The WizDome

After dinner, I ventured out into the backyard to my tree house. It is famous throughout the neighborhood as the "WizDome." My dad built it when I was still a "twinkle" in my parents' eyes, he once told me. He knew that someday he would want to share the world of astronomy with his kids.

The WizDome is a magical place for hanging out. It is built in "Luna," a magnificent 300-year-old tree. My ancestors planted her to honor the founding of Iridescent Village. An ancient legend says that she is a tree of light. Sailors in years past reported that she guided them home on dark and foggy nights by the light from her massive limbs. Local scientists have not yet been able to prove that she is luminescent, but I think that she glows from time to time.

Climbing into the branches of this magical tree is like entering another universe. This is the special playground of the *cocuyos*. Vines of moonflowers that open at dusk encase the tree trunk. When the *cocuyos* come out to play, it's a magical night kingdom.

"Hi-ya, Luna." I gazed up into the canopy of leaves waving gently in the twilight breeze. I felt the mist on my face as I began to climb the winding staircase of wood to my hideaway.

I stood in front of the solar-powered locks on the door and watched them unlock as the sun sank beneath the horizon. Then I opened the door and walked inside. My little frog, "Coqui,"

 greeted me from his bubbling pond ecosystem. He smiled at me. At least I think he did. Then, walking around the stone pond, I greeted the *cocuyos*. That's when I heard the first creak. I listened silently to try to figure out where the

creak had come from.

"Coookyee," Coqui croaked.

Startled, I jumped four stars in the air. "Shhhhh," I said, holding a finger to my lips. I listened again. Nothing. Then, Creeeeaaaaak. My eyes opened wide. I looked at the roof of the tree house and saw the back of Burst's tennis shoe as it passed by. Smiling, I opened one of the ceiling trap doors and in crashed Burst, landing on the wooden floor.

"Yeouch!," he said rubbing his bum.

"Ah-ha! I caught ya'! So, why were you sneaking about up in Luna's branches?" I asked, grinning.

"Lums, how come I am known as the fastest kid in town, but you always seem to be one step ahead of me? Do you have night vision now that you're shiny?"

"Not night vision, just excellent hearing from my mom's Jupiter Nutrition bars," I replied. I began to water the moonflowers, which were just opening their petals on the windowsill.

"Right," Burst said skeptically.

"Your mom told me you were out here in the Dome," Burst said.

"The WizDome," I corrected.

Burst studied me closely. He walked around me in a circle, squinting and blinking his eyes open and shut.

"You still look funny. Did you swallow some cocuyos or something?"

"Those little guys? Nope. I don't eat them because their taillights tell me that they are bioluminescent and have a nasty taste. That's why they light up, ya' know, to tell predators that they taste yucky."

"Thank you, Miss Oxford Dictionary," Burst said. "So what's with this new experiment you hinted at earlier?"

"Well, I've discovered that we can all glow by using some special tools," I explained.

Burst's eyebrows shot up a few inches. "*What*

are you talking about? What is glow?" he asked.

I stepped up to my podium and delivered my State of the Glow address, "**Burst, when we glow, we are in touch with our natural capabilities, inner balance, wholeness, creativity, wisdom, and health**," I said, with a wave of my hand.

Hearing no response, I turned around to find Burst chewing on an old star fruit tart, making faces and having a frog conversation with Coqui. He glanced up at me and asked with his mouth full, "Hey, Lums, you got any more of these tarts, or how 'bout some ice cream?"

Hmm, just as I'd thought, I was going to need a different angle. I paused for a moment. Then it blasted into my mind like a rocket at take-off. Ice Cream would get his attention and imagination going! I would show Burst how to turn on his glow by using some *Mind Travel.* I would be his glow guide. Since Burst loves ice cream, the experience of it in his imagination was bound to make his glow bigger.

"Burst, how 'bout I show you how to experience the smell and taste of ice cream without even having to find some?" I asked.

"Show me the way, Lums," Burst said with a smile as he quickly swallowed the lump of tart.

"Great! I bet I can make you *think* dessert faster than we can find some."

"*Think* dessert? I'm pretty sure I like *tasting* dessert more than thinking it." Burst said.

"Trust me, I think you'll enjoy this little experiment," I said running to get him a stack of National Geode Starlight magazines to sit on.

"Stuart T. Turnsey," I said, "Sit here, and close your eyes."

"Miss Oxford's getting a little bossy," Burst muttered to himself. But he sat down.

"Now, close your eyes and play along."

Got Glow?

Chapter Nine

"Burst, imagine that you are in the Milky Way Galaxy Ice Cream shop. They have just set down the 'Big Dipper' sundae in front of you. Smell the two scoops of planetary blueberry ice cream." I paused to let the vision sink in.

"Can you see it? Can you smell it?" I asked, studying his face carefully.

"Um, hmm," he mumbled.

"Now, picture the rest of the sundae: one scoop of Mars dusty road is deliciously in the center, a scoop of Venus bubblegum with pink morsels of peppermint inside, some fizzy, bubbling space foam on top." Burst's smile was growing bigger by the second. "Finally there's cherry meteorite candy filling the craters along the sides. On the very top, there is a single candied star fruit, and the entire sundae is dribbling with chocolate stars and orbited by swirls of caramel. Can you see it?"

"Yep," Burst squeaked.

I started to whisper. "Now imagine that you

are picking up your spoon and digging into this amazing sundae. There is ice cream falling off as it gets to your mouth. Open your mouth, and feel that *fizzy* space foam tingling on your tongue. Taste the Mars Dusty Road chocolate bits and marshmallow crème. It's the best ice cream you have ever tasted. Your mouth is soooo happy," I said speaking slowly and enunciating the words, as I waved away a stream of glowing bubbles. *That's interesting, I thought. I would have to investigate* glowing bubbles *later.*

I watched his face break into a fabulously goofy grin. His eyes were still closed, and he was leaning forward as if to take a bite. He was definitely getting in touch with his glow! I could see it hovering around his head. *Mind Travel* had worked for him too! I pulled my Light Journal out of my pocket and began to jot down some notes.

In my normal voice, I announced, "Burst, you can open your eyes now."

His eyes popped opened just as the magazines toppled into a pile and scattered on the floor. He sat there looking dazed, but radically content.

"Whoa, that was some ice cream! Way cool and yummy, too!" Burst said.

"Is your mouth watering?" I asked.

"Yeah, it is the weirdest thing. I could really taste it! Every bite! That was great!" he said, with a gigantic grin. "Want to swing from the moonflower vines?" he asked.

I ignored him and dug around in the 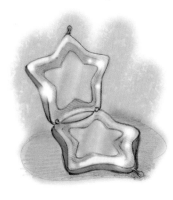 WizDome's celestial chest to come up with a **Reflective Detective**. I held it in front of his face. "Look here, and tell me what you see."

Burst studied his reflection, and his eyes opened very wide. "I have that look, that shiny look like you did! Sweet..." he said turning his head from side to side.

"This is what I have been trying to tell you. This stuff works! You can glow too, just like me and every other kid. I just helped you to experience your glow by using your imagination through **Mind Travel**. When you felt stellar, your glow got bigger," I said smiling victoriously.

"You see, we have the power to change the way we think or feel about anything by using our imagination."

I waved away a gigantic bubble and stuck out my hand. "Let me introduce myself. I am Lumina Osity, and I got glow. And you are? . . ."

"I'm, Burst, and I got glow?"

"Exactly! You *have* got it! *Every kid's got glow*. You see how incredibly powerful it is to know this?"

Burst bounced up and started to jog around the WizDome. "I'm glowing, I'm glowing, I feel so good I'm glowing," he chanted. "This is soooo radically sweet!" But I wasn't listening. I was distracted by effervescent bubbles. I could hardly see Burst as he celebrated. *I don't remember having a* bubble *machine.* Shooting stars! *Now I had a* bubble *mystery to solve.*

Bubbles

"Burst!" I shouted, trying to peek through the bubbly air. "Are you still there?" Bubbles were shooting out of the branches, inside and outside, filling up the entire dome.

Not hearing an immediate answer, I did a nosedive to the floor and began to crawl in his direction. In a minute, I bumped right into his leg.

"Lums!" he said excitedly, "Are we about to take off? What is all this?" He was looking wildly around the room. He swished by me and did a SLaM dUNK in the air.

"Grab a *cocuyo* lantern, Burst. We've got to go up and investigate," I said.

We stood on the branch table and he boosted me through the trap door, and then climbed up after me.

"Luna," I whispered. "Are you OK?" We climbed out on the thickest tree branch, which glowed a brilliant sun-yellow-orange. Glittering bubbles appeared to be oozing out of her branches in sparkling spheres. It was suddenly very quiet, and you could hear the chorus of crickets begin their nightly serenade. I looked over my shoulder to see what had happened to Burst.

He was staring at me, his mouth gaping open. "Are you talking to a tree?"

"Don't you see what's going on here?" I said, impatiently. "It's Luna! The legend is true! She is a tree of light, and she is glowing bubbles!"

Burst rolled his eyes. "Another Lumina factoid for the collection," he said shaking his head in amazement.

A *cocuyo* floated by encased in a glitter bubble. "Catch that *cocuyo*, Burst!" I yelled.

With his lightning reflexes, he reached up and popped the bubble, setting the *cocuyo* free.

"Luna is glowing because of all of the power we generated inside the WizDome! The more we used our imaginations and **amplified** our glow, the more Luna **amplified** hers." *Wait a minute.* Glow Note: *Explore* glow **amplification.** I was so excited that I ran down the branch and gave the tree a galactic hug.

Burst and I sat down on the branch and hung the *cocuyo* lanterns on some tiny branches above our heads. We silently watched the bubbles sparkle and float for a couple of minutes. It had been a Glow-rific evening.

Our Secret

"Hey guys, you up there?" called our friend Ivy through the trapdoor. She was standing in a pile of squishy bubble residue and gazing up at us from below.

"There's some kind of bubble machine blow up goin' on down here," she called.

I glanced at Burst. I had forgotten that I had asked Ivy to come by to drop off some set design plans for the next school theater production. I was going to have Ori look them over.

"Ivy girl you gotta get up here, we've just discov. . . ." I clamped my hand over Burst's mouth, cutting him off.

Then I crawled over to the trap door and peered through it. Ivy was standing below looking up.

"Guys, I gotta run, can I just drop these plans here on the table?" she asked.

"Super!" I said.

"I'll catch ya tomorrow at school, you're lookin' kinda different. And, are your *cocuyos* doing overtime or something? The tree is really bright tonight." Ivy said.

But, without waiting for an answer, she did a salute and headed out the door and down the tree steps.

"Whew, that was a close one," I said crawling back to sit next to Burst.

"I can't wait to tell everyone on the hockey team. This is incredible. With glow power, we will win every game from now on."

"Uh, Burst, not so fast," I said hesitating. "I think we need to think this through first. I want everyone to know, but I have some final experiments I need to make. Will you hang up your skates and keep this secret for a few days?"

"OK, if you say so, Lums, but I want to be in on the action once we start showing this around."

"Deal.   Now we both have a monstrous maximus test on Master Minds tomorrow. "Ready to study?" I asked.

The last of the bubbles floated away.   We climbed back through the trap door and sat down by the light of Luna's branches to study.

Later that evening, I watched Burst leave through the mist to his house.   I sat there and made tiny notes in my Light Journal, which still had some sticky bubbles stuck to it.   I could hear my dad calling from the Light House.   It was time for bed.

A Visit from Leonardo

Chapter Twelve

The next day, I blasted to school in seconds using my wheelie rocket shoes, arriving in a bright cloud of glitter. The village's school, Galileo Elementary, is a lab school for the university. It was designed with a science twist. Its construction is supernova sweet. The massive steel and glass walls are like the walls in a space station. The school is shaped like an octagon with a courtyard in the center where we eat lunch. Trees and giant flowers burst from planet-shaped pots forming a solar system of green stuff. A sundial keeps time in the center of everything. Our playground is like a trip to space camp with flying satellite swings, simulator chambers and bouncing rocket ships.

I tapped my rocket wheelies twice and screeched to a halt just before the bike rack.

Omnia, my next door neighbor, was putting away her bike.

"Lumina, sweeeet shoes, where did you get them?" she asked.

"I made them myself," I declared proudly.

"Girlfriend, your stars are twinkling today, where'd you get all that sparkle?" she said, looking at me.

"I've really been getting into the star homework," I said, not wanting to share too much too soon. Then, Omnia and I walked together down the hall to our class.

Going to Classroom Number Eight is so much fun that you hardly know time exists. Mr. Semple, our teacher, defines intergalactic coolness. He is like one of those "mad scientist" college professors, you know. He sometimes even wears a white lab coat and has crazy, wild hair and big spectacles that slide down his nose. He designs lessons that defy gravity, and teaches them with over-the-top excitement. This month we are studying Master Minds. Mr. Semple teaches this class so we can study interesting people who have majorly influenced our planet.

When Omnia and I got to the classroom, we were surprised to find the entire class standing in a group around the door peeking inside and whispering. Curious, we squeezed through the group to see what was up. A strange man with a feather hat, long ponytail and a flowing cape was writing scribbles all over the chalkboard with a great flourish!

"Oh, no, Omnia exclaimed, "*Not a substitute* on the day of our Master Minds test!"

"We need a plan and fast!" I whispered. I gestured for everyone to form a huddle. We all started talking at once.

I jumped to the middle of the circle and held

up my hands, "Wait! I think somebody must solve this mystery, close up. What if we send someone to introduce Class Number Eight to the mystery guy at the board?" I suggested.

"I'm game!" Burst volunteered.

"Try not to mess it up," Magnitude bossed.

Before we could explain more, Burst was already tiptoeing toward the front of the room. We all silently tiptoed behind him in a clump. When he stopped, we stopped. When he went, we went. Burst approached the mystery man and quietly touched his sleeve. In a whirl, the man turned around and bellowed, "*Buon Giorno*, Class Number Eight! *Atenzione!*"

Leaping Light Beams! Our eyes opened wide, and the entire class gasped as Burst fell backwards into our circle. It was Mr. Semple dressed up like Leonardo da Vinci !!

Well, there ya' go,-just another day in Classroom Number Eight.

Buon Giorno
is
"good morning"
in Italian.
Atenzione
is
"attention"
in Italian.

Mind Stretching

Classroom Number Eight was once the school theater, but had recently been transformed into the third-grade classroom. Mr. Semple teaches from center stage with spotlights and a curtain. And today with his artist's hat and colorful costume, he brought the old theater back to life. Our desks, which are actually graphing tables, are arranged in pairs in semi-circular rows in front of center stage. Every student has his or her own mini-spotlight and tall chair. The ceiling has skylights in the shape of stars. There are remote-controlled shades that lighten or darken the room for different effects.

As we all wiggled around putting our stuff away, Mr. Semple da Vinci announced loudly in an Italian accent, "Looks like this class needs a little settling down. Today is the day of our Master

Minds test. In preparation, we are going to do some MIND STRETCHING. This is a two-part tool that gets your mind and body connected so you are feeling ready to think."

"Ewww, gross," Magnitude stuck out her tongue and made a disgusted face.

"Shouldn't take you long, huh, Mags?" Burst joked.

Mr. Semple da Vinci continued, pointing one finger in the air, "Who was Da Vinci?"

"A guy who makes noodles?" someone called out. The class snickered.

"Not that Da Vinci, but *grazie*. Leonardo da Vinci was a well-known, brilliant scientist, inventor and artist from Italy. He painted this magnificent fresco," Mr. Semple da Vinci said, pointing one of his jewel-ringed fingers to the painting on the wall. Our friend Leonardo was an

Grazie means "thank you" in Italian.

expert in MIND STRETCHING and the inspiration for what we are about to learn," he said.

"Oooh, I'm starting to get a headache already," Magnitude whined, holding her forehead.

Burst rolled his eyes.

Mr. Semple da Vinci dramatically unrolled a gigantic map of the brain, and spread it out on the floor for all of us to see.

"OK, geniuses, pick a colorful brain cell, or neuron, to stand on. Neurons are made up of three major parts. The cell body, or soma, is the central operating station of the neuron. The dendrites are little fingers that accept information into the soma. That information then travels down a branch called an axon."

"So, Mr. Semple, is it like these little dudes are having conversations?" somebody asked.

"Si, **molto bene**.

The neurons send information between each other by using little chemicals called neurotransmitters. The neurotransmitters get the information from the axon of one neuron and carry it across a bridge called a synapse to the dendrite of the next neuron," Mr. Semple da Vinci replied with a big smile on his face.

Molto bene means "very good" in Italian.

"Cool game," Burst said.

"Hey, Stuart Turnsey, dial 'L' for Loser," Magnitude called out, making an "L" sign with her finger and pointing it at Burst. The twins giggled in unison.

"Hey, Wanda. . ." Burst began, but was interrupted by Mr. Semple da Vinci who began to toss colored caps out to all of us. "The green hats will be the dendrites, the yellow hats will be the neurotransmitters and the blue hats will be the axons," he said. We each put on a hat and waited.

Burst, who was standing next to Magnitude, called out, glancing in her direction, "Uh oh, watch out for short circuits."

The whole class began to laugh. Mr. Semple da Vinci continued, "You will send messages to each other in order to form a thought that might help you feel better-prepared for the test. The neurotransmitters will pick a word from the axons and carry it over to the dendrites who will assemble the message on the board. Each person should announce their word when it is their turn. Let's see how fast we can make the connections work."

"What if we don't exactly connect with everyone?" Burst asked looking at Magnitude.

"It is in the best interest of all of you to think and link powerful positive thoughts.

Neurons *that fire together, wire together. The more you fire positive thoughts, the more positive you will feel,"* Mr. Semple da Vinci answered.

I couldn't believe my ears! This was amazing! Mr. Semple da Vinci was speaking the language of glow. He was explaining everything I had already discovered! I immediately pulled out my Light Journal and took a Glow Note. As I was writing, Mr. Semple da Vinci walked to center stage and opened the curtains with a flourish, his cape swinging. He turned to the class and said, "Are you ready?" We nodded. Then, let part one of MIND STRETCHING begin."

Wiring Together

The next few minutes were pretty zero-gravity amazing. The class mysteriously became a symphony of cooperation. The neurotransmitters picked up the words and gracefully danced them over to the dendrites who carefully arranged them on a giant gold-framed board. The dendrites seemed to know just which word went with which neurotransmitter. As we moved, the connections gathered speed. Soon it went from outside our brains to inside our brains and became something we really knew. When we finished, the following words were written in glittering letters on the board:

My brain is an information super highway.

I looked around the room. It had worked! The class had definitely formed a team and had settled down.

"Mr. Semple da Vinci?" I asked. "If our brain processes just about 12,000 thoughts a minute, how is just one thought going to prepare us for the test?"

"Good question," Mr. Semple da Vinci replied. Then his voice became very low and mysterious, as he raised his finger and said:

It is because repetition is the key to mastery of thought. We must repeat, repeat, repeat in order to form new networks of thought in the brain.

"That's another Glow Note. I did that when I *flushed it*!" I said out loud.

The whole class looked at me. Magnitude made a face and said, "That is serious gross, 'Osity. Hey, *grossosity*, new word for you."

This time, I *flushed* her words right out of my mind before they could take hold.

Mr. Semple da Vinci ignored us and continued his lesson. "Class, please return to your desks. Next is part two of MIND STRETCHING. I need to show you more about how to get ready for the test," he said.

Excitedly, we returned to our desks and sat down.   I glanced at my current desk partner,  Shantanu who was smiling as usual. Shantanu is new to Galileo Elementary this year. His family just moved from India to do research at the university. He's an interesting sort of kid who is into music. I've seen him and some other kids in the school jamming at recess and making really cool sounds. I don't know him very well. He's a bit of a mystery 'cause he's always smiling and seems to have mastered his cool.

I was distracted by some faint swishing coming from the skylight above. Looking up, I saw a swarm of *cocuyos* doing somersaults like they were trying to get inside with us. I made a motion for them to hit the road. I looked over at Shantanu who was grinning knowingly.

"Friends of yours?" he asked.

"Um, yep, but friends with lousy timing," I explained. But, I was surprised that he had asked.

Looking down at my desk I found a funny-looking pair of glasses. They looked a little like safety goggles only more high-tech. Colorful blinking lights ran in a circle around the frames.

Tiny earphones were attached, and they fit just inside our ears when we put them on. We snapped them into place, and the lenses became our screen. A little graph entitled "Feelings-o-meter" popped up in red light. It seemed to be a sort of monitor for our feelings because it immediately told me how I was feeling. In my ears, I heard: Calm 52, Curiosity 100!

Mr. Semple da Vinci asked us to quiet down and in the same moment the lights in the room went out!

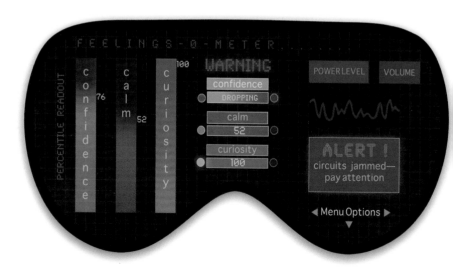

VR Mind Voyage

Chapter Fifteen

"Mind boggling!"

"Unreal!"

"Something else!"

"Score!"

The whole class was buzzing with excitement. Inside the glasses, a brain that looked so real you could almost touch it, popped up in front of us. It was rotating in slow motion. Purplish gray, it had fluorescent lights lighting up all over from the inside. It looked like a thundercloud with lightning at night.

"Wow, Mr. S, you brought virtual reality to the classroom. This is as cool as the virtual soccer game I played at the kids' museum last week," Omnia said.

"*Molto bene*. Now, my genius class, stand by for a *VR Mind Voyage*. Pay attention to what you see and hear as you journey inside the brain."

As we watched it rotate, a voice boomed. . .

Neurons, the brain uses to think
Relax, focus and create links
This opens your mind
So you can find
You are the master of magnificent things

The Feelings-o-meter popped up and announced in my ear: Confidence 100 percent. Target reached. "Bring it on," I heard someone in the class call out.

But there was no time to think or feel, because this ride was taking off. The brain stopped its rotation and sucked us in! My hands sprang to my chair and gripped tightly. The brain world had hills and curves of bumpy gray matter. We gathered speed and began to race along the roadways. We traveled up bridges, around corners and through narrow passageways. It felt as if we might be the signals between the neurons themselves!

Suddenly, we entered a dark, dark tunnel.

There was no light at all. I panicked and on the screen flashed the Feelings-o-meter. **Warning! Warning! Confidence dropping: 50 percent.** The warning flashed red.

Then my journey came to a halt. The Feelings-o-meter flashed on the screen: **Circuits jammed. Not enough power to continue.** Then the voice boomed: **"Remember what you know."**

"What?" I sputtered.

"Remember what you know!" the voice insisted.

"What do I know?" I shouted. Then, a Glow Thought popped into my head: My brain is an information superhighway. I silently thanked my lucky stars for Mr. Semple da Vinci.

The Feelings-o-meter flashed green: Target Reached. Confidence rising.

The tunnel and darkness disappeared as our journey fired up again and we sped along through the hills. After a minute, the journey ended.

Whew! I sat at my desk feeling proud and

calm. That was quite a ride. I pulled off the glasses and looked around the room. The class buzzed with energy and confidence. Everyone talked excitedly about their experience. Then I noticed it! Well, launch me a rocket, *THE ENTIRE CLASS WAS GLOWING!* That confirmed it: **Everyone has the power to glow.** Then, I thought to myself, *VR Mind Voyage produces glow?— Investigate later!*

"Hey, Mr. S. pass out that test already, I am ready to rumble," Burst called out.

"What a class of geniuses. *The mind is the brain in action. Now you all understand a little better that your brain is plastic. It can and does remodel itself, often within a very short period of time.* Grab your pens, the test is your canvas, paint me a picture!"

Pool of Confidence

As he passed out the test, I peeked around the edge of my desk to see Shantanu. He looked the same as usual, sitting there quietly with a smile on his face and drumming his fingers like the desk was a drum. Ever so often he would pause and write something on scraps of paper. It looked like he was writing notes—you know, of the musical kind.

I took a deep breath. I was still feeling the effects from the *VR Mind Voyage.* Burst and I had studied so much. I was sure that there was nothing on that test that I didn't already know. I sat there in a regular pool of confidence, sipping my lemonade, floating on my lifesaver of knowledge. Nope, there would be no surprising me today. I was ready!

Mr. Semple da Vinci gave us the cue to

begin. I glanced over the questions. *Shooting stars!* Immediately my heart sank because I found them far from simple. We were supposed to match up the famous Master Minds with their discoveries.

I felt the panic rise, the doubt began inching in like a wiggly wormy. I started to sweat. My lifesaver of knowledge sprang a leak, and I felt myself slowly sinking into a pool of *Mind Muck*. I couldn't remember ***anything!*** Did Einstein invent electricity? What did Dr. Martin Luther King Jr. discover? I grabbed my desk. I wanted to fall into a black hole again. What was I going to do?

Cocuyos through the Window?

Chapter Seventeen

I sat there feeling **space rocks** gather in my stomach. In panic, my eyes darted to Shantanu. He was calmly creating his masterpiece! Looking closer, I caught a glimmer of glow shining ever so lightly around him. I studied him for a minute and then suddenly, without thinking, I shouted, "I got it! The glow. . ."

"Everything OK, Lumina?" Mr. Semple da Vinci interrupted.

"Uh, yeah, um fine, Mr. S.," I stammered, surprised that I had announced my thought out loud. I quickly scrambled to look busy. I decided to chat with Shantanu later. Then I turned back to my test.

As Mr. Semple da Vinci walked away, *cocuyos* started flying in through the window and surrounding my desk. Good Great Glitter!

They found a way in!

As they fluttered around, glitter dusted my desk. I glanced around the room to see who was looking. Everyone but Shantanu was busy with their test. Shantanu was gesturing with his hands, nodding and smiling to the *cocuyos*!

"Shantanu!" I whispered in exasperation, "*What* are you doing?"

"You better listen to these little dudes. They're pretty smart," he whispered back.

But I had no time to answer. I was being surrounded by a symphony of blinking. They seemed to be trying to tell me something very important. Meanwhile Mr. Semple da Vinci was writing the time left on the chalkboard.

Glow Blinks

Chapter Eighteen

As fast as a shooting star, I turned back to the *cocuyos*. Looking closer, I saw that their blinks were all lighting up together. I blinked a few times myself. It was a code!!! I took my pencil and wrote it down.

•—• (pause) • (pause) •—•• (pause) •— (pause) —•—

Staring at the page, I could hardly believe my eyes. The *cocuyos* were blinking Morse code!

My dad used that all the time to talk around the world on his radios. I wrote the code and matched up the letters. Leaping light beams! I was glad that I had paid attention.

Morse code is a method for transmitting letters using sequences of short and long elements.

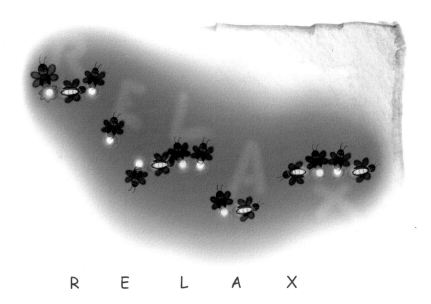

R   E   L   A   X

As soon as I wrote the last letter, the *cocuyos* did a little dance and swarmed out the nearest window. I jumped up.

"R-E-L-A-X!" A *Glow Thought*!" I announced pointing a finger of discovery in the air. I started moon dancing. The whole class turned to stare at me.

"Uh,...sorry?" I sheepishly apologized. My moon dancing still landed me and my test in the Chill-Out Station.

Invisible Message

In the Chill-Out Station I took the Glow Thought "RELAX" and experimented. First, I closed my eyes. Then I wiggled my body and told it to be still, finally adding some deep breaths to the mixture. I was starting to feel floaty, like when I tried the zero gravity chambers at space camp. My mind slowed, and my thoughts cleared. This time it wasn't as hard as before. Maybe the more you practiced Glow Thoughts, the easier it would be to glow.

I felt my glow get brighter as I turned my attention full speed ahead on the test. I opened my eyes and started to write, and watched the clouds of glitter scatter as I wrote.

After the test, when I had thawed out, I went back to my desk. Most of the class was already at lunch. My desk was covered with a pile of glitter. As I brushed it aside, a laser pen fell onto the floor. Picking it up, I saw there was a mini-note attached. It read:

Shine Me Under The Desk

O-kaaaaaaayyyyyy.   Weirder things have happened. I leaned under the desk and turned it on. As the light shined under my desk, I saw the following words appear:

Glow sharing at sundial NOW!
— Shantanu

Good Great Glitter!!   He had used invisible ink, and I got it. I immediately stuck the laser pen in my pocket and rushed as fast as a shooting star outside.

The Simulation Chamber

Chapter Twenty

I ran to the sundial. I could hear some kind of unfamiliar rap music. A lunchtime show was going on.

Pushing my way to the front of the crowd, I could not believe my eyes. There was Shantanu jamming away and doing some out-of-this-world dancing. The *cocuyos* were his back-up blinkers! The glow was so bright that I had to pull out my Flaming Star shades! The kids gathered around were also starting to glow a little. I gasped. The glow was contagious out here just like in the classroom. My curiosity shot off like a rocket, I couldn't stand it any more. I had to know NOW, not later. I grabbed Shantanu's arm, unplugging him from the show. We jetted across the playground into a simulation chamber. I slammed the door behind us.

Shantanu was grinning, "Dude, what is up?! he asked.

"Dude," I mimicked, "You are glowing so much I had to apply the shades. Let's do a little rewind just for fun. First, you spoke to the *cocuyos*. Then, you left this secret invisible message that I deciphered with a laser pen. Next, I find you, the One-Guy Jamming Show. And, finally, you are glowing like a solar flare. What I want to know is, do you know what I know? Let's have it." I crossed my arms and leaned back against the wall.

Suddenly the whole simulation chamber was activated. The noise of take off switched on, and the chamber started to shake and rumble. I looked around frantically for something to hold onto. Shantanu calmly reached out and pressed the simulation abort button.

"Uh, thank you." I said rolling my eyes at the ceiling.

"Sure, anytime," Shantanu answered.

"Soooooooo?" I waited.

"Listen dude, this is not rocket science. Here's how it all sounds. When I came to this country I was more than a little ... freaked out, shall we say? *Here* is, uh, different, from *there* in India and I started to feel a little bummed," he said.

"You? Bummed?" I asked, disbelievingly.

"I carry on. Soon I discovered that I could feel better if I started jammin' to my tunes and movin' along."

"And that's when you discovered glow?"

"No," Shantanu raised his eyebrows and looked at me.

"Uh, carry on," I said.

"So I started jamming whenever I felt bummed." Shantanu said.

"And that's when you discovered glow?"

"No, that's when I started feeling good," he said.

So, **WHAT ABOUT THE GLOW?**" I exploded.

"Dude, it's simple. I've *always* had the glow. When I was feeling bummed, the glow would shrink. When I started relaxing and feeling good while jammin', I started amplifying the glow again. So I decided to call it Om Jammin," he said.

Om is an ancient sound that creates a peaceful feeling.

"R-r-r-right. **Amplification**, again!" I said. My mind started whirling. I reached for my Light Journal and began to compute.

"Oh, the possibilities of glow! Shantanu, you have a stellar formula! Supernova swee .... !"

"Whoa, let's *feel* it, not think it." Shantanu jumped in front of me and held out his hand. I gotta give you a little demo. Then he flipped the anti-gravity switch, and the floor beneath my feet disappeared as I began to float through the air.

Gravity is the force that holds people and objects on the earth. Anti-gravity is a chamber that takes the force, or pull of gravity away so that you can float freely through the air. It is used often to train astronauts before they go into space where there is no gravitational pull.

Om Jammin

I started moving slowly and doing somersaults. I was standing on my head when Shantanu called out.

"Listen up, girl." Shantanu pulled his music pod out of his pocket and turned it on. "Close your eyes, and just *feel* the beat."

Shantanu adjusted the speakers and instantaneously a thunderous beat sent shock waves throughout the chamber. I closed my eyes and didn't feel much to begin with. Then it started in my toe. It wanted to wiggle. Then I felt it in my legs. *They* wanted to wiggle. Soon, my whole body joined in, and I wiggled all over. So I wiggled and wiggled and wiggled some more. I popped open an eye to see where Shantanu was. He was spinning around in his own world. *Great, I thought, he's no help. Must be nice.*

Distracted, I lost a little of my wiggle. Then, out of nowhere, the *cocuyos* showed up.

"What do ya' have to say this time?" I asked.

More code ...

R E L A X

They immediately blinked out their message again. Oh, a rerun. Thanks guys, I'm working on it. They seemed to smile and then flew off. I closed my eyes again, took a deep breath and *relaxed*.

This time the music filled the air with rhythm I could almost touch. A tidal wave of sound washed over me. In my mind, I began to move and float and feel free as my imagination turned up the volume. I imagined a train of elephants marching in. Shantanu was riding on the lead elephant. Many colored flower petals began to fall from the ceiling. The elephants were marching and dancing in rhythm to the music, shuffling and kicking toward the Taj Mahal.

There were people dancing and whirling around
with colored scarves. Even the *cocuyos* were
dancing to the rhythm. Dada-boom. Dada-boom.
Dada-boom-boom-boom.

I smiled. I felt weightless and happy. I could have floated there for a very long time, but the music stopped suddenly. Crash! I fell to the floor with a big thud. I opened my eyes to see that Shantanu had flipped the anti-gravity switch. He looked at me and put on his shades.

"Whew, **amplification of glow** achieved."

I squinted at him. He was pretty bright himself. "One last teeny question," I said, pinching my fingers together to show teeny. "Tell more about this 'Om' sound," I said.

"Did you feel happy? Peaceful? Calm? Chilled-out?" Shantanu asked. I nodded. "That, dude, is what the sound of Om does, and Om Jammin takes you there," he said.

I pulled out my Light Journal to capture Om Jammin. Glow Note:

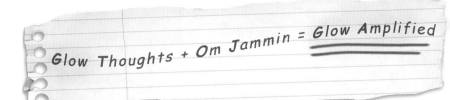

Glow Thoughts + Om Jammin = Glow Amplified

Fixing and Mixing

Before I left school that day, I called a WizDome meeting and invited Shantanu and Burst. They would be coming over at twilight to discuss the power of glow and our next steps.

As I walked home, the wind swirled around me. I had to accelerate the wheelie rocket shoe in order to make it home in a flash. As I was taking off, a piece of paper from out of nowhere slapped me right on the face. Pulling it off, I read "School Science Fair Competition." Hm, I made a mental note to check that out later and stuffed it into my Voyager Pac.

Reaching the Light House, I called "hello" to my mom and blasted up the 68 winding steps to my CS Observatory. I was determined to use the Glow Notes and get to the bottom of glow once and for all. I threw open the door. Just as I ran into the room, the windows also flew open. On the way to my Research and Development table, I tripped over *Shimmer's* cage, and out he scooted with the speed of light colliding with my stereo. The music was ignited, and Swan Lake filled the room.

Oh well, I thought, letting him go. I had other things on my mind. The observatory was suddenly a whirlwind of energy. Glitter dust clouds filled the air. I rushed around trying to catch random constellation drawings and notes that had taken flight. *Shimmer* huddled in the corner shivering with chattering teeth. Just as I pushed through the strong wind to reach the windows, the *cocuyos* flew in! They were smiling and instantly began to choreograph the music. I

Swan Lake is a famous classical music piece by the Russian composer, Tchaikovsky. A Japanese scientist, Dr. Masaru Emoto, has shown that certain music such as Swan Lake has healing benefit when listened to. I play it and feel good while listening to it.

slammed each window shut and turned around to face the commotion.

As the glitter settled, I pushed through the clutter and got busy. I pulled my Light Journal out and collected all the Glow Notes from inside. I stuck them on my glittering fluorescent chalkboard. The *cocuyos* hovered overhead to watch what I was doing. Next, I grabbed some beakers, test tubes, graduated cylinders and valves. I assembled some petri dishes and colorful liquids from the shelf. Hm, I thought to myself. Some special kind of spice was still missing. I dove into my treasure chest of supplies and came out with it: my Space Pod! It was filled with comet dust, moon pebbles, solar rays, and liquefied starlight. Perfect! That ought to be enough to start with.

Looking up at the *cocuyos*, I said, "OK guys,

make yourselves useful. I'll direct. You mix." And so, with the *cocuyos* as my assistants and the Glow Notes as my guide, we began to formulate.

Glow Blast

Chapter Twenty-Three

We started to mix, mingle and formulate the biggest concoction ever imagined. I stood like the director of my own orchestra. I pointed. They poured. In went a pinch of relaxation. In went the essence of Om Jammin. In went a cube of *Mind Travel*, and a vial of repetition. I closed my eyes at one point and added a deep breath.

The beaker was beginning to shake and rumble like an earthquake. Steam and colored glitter bubbles rose up and spread around the room. Oh no, I was beginning to think my solution had a problem!

Fizzy ooze sloshed and poured over the sides of the beaker! I snapped on my safety goggles and passed some tiny goggles out to the *cocuyos*. I rolled up my sleeves to top it all off. It was time to add the final, but most important, most basic ingredient, a sprinkling of Glow Thoughts. Each *cocuyo* dropped one of their Glow Thoughts into the beaker as well.

As the last Glow Thought floated down into the bubbling soup, a gigantic bubble began to grow out of the beaker until it was as big as a full moon! My eyes opened wide and then I squeezed them shut and grabbed onto the edge of the table. Kaaaaaa-BOOOOM! Thwaaaash! There was an explosion as big as an earthquake, tidal wave, tornado and hurricane all rolled into one! It was so powerful that my legs were lifted

out from under me and were propelled straight behind as I held tight to the table. Then, it was quiet. There was no noise. Only silence.

I slowly opened my eyes one by one, and was blinded by the sheer sight of GLOW!

I could hear my mom call from downstairs. "Lumina, everything OK up there?"

"Yes, Mom, no worries," I called.

I got up to investigate. *Cocuyos* were plastered to the wall with iridescent sparkling goo of all colors. Shimmy was holding his eyes and peeking through his paws. Copernicus had an arm folded across his forehead and was floating to the bottom of the tank.

As I unstuck the *cocuyos* from the goo, it came to me. Too many ingredients mixed together at one time had produced overwhelming glow power. Better to make the concoctions into small formulas, and to make them one at a time.

Formulas

The full moon was beginning to rise, a brilliant orange ball of light. The wind had transformed into a tickling breeze. Luna was gently swaying her branches as I climbed up to the WizDome. I was near stumbling with the weight of Voyager Pac, the formulas safely inside, and all my charts and plans.

Inside the WizDome, I was surprised to see a table filled with my mom's best food art. There was a tall tower of moonbeam cakes, shiny glazed star fruit tarts, spicy barbequed Saturn ring onions and astronomical stellar smoothies with blueberry star cubes inside. Yum, yum and yum!

I began my daily routine. I fed Coqui and herded the cocuyos into their lanterns. Burst and Shantanu were hollering Tarzan-like calls. I ran to the window to watch. They were swinging from vines through the trees.

"Hey, Shanti, get this," Burst called, doing a somersault in the air.

"Dude, check this out," Shantanu flipped over a cluster of branches, busting some moves from his Om Jam.

"*Excusez-moi*, are we going to get glowing or what?" I asked, tapping my foot on the floor.

They swung on in.

Excusez-moi is French for "Excuse me"

"Sweet! Lums, your mom has the greatest lineup," Burst said staring googley-eyed at the table.

They munched, I talked. "Here is the thing of it. You guys have helped me discover three things of galactic importance: **The first thing is that glow exists. The second thing is that everybody has it. The third thing is that you can make glow bigger by using glow amplification formulas.**

Burst sputtered and spit astronomical shake all over us. "Are you sure about that one?" He said wiping his mouth with the back of his hand, "I mean, have you watched Magnitude and her team in action? No way!"

Rolling my eyes and wiping blueberries from my face, I replied, "I think that everybody has the *glow*, but may have just forgotten where they put it."

All of a sudden, the *cocuyo* lanterns lit up wildly and began to shake. Burst opened their door and let them out. They danced and began their code blinking.

•–• (pause)	•• (pause)	–•• (pause)	•••• (pause)	–	––– (pause)	–•
R	I	G	H	T	O	N
•–• (pause)	•• (pause)	–•• (pause)	•••• (pause)	–	––– (pause)	–•
R	I	G	H	T	O	N

"They're saying, 'Right on, right on,'" I translated for Burst.

"See, those little dudes really get it. After all, they've spent eons *glowing* their *glow*,"

Shantanu said.

I jumped back up to explain more. "Once you know glow, you always Glow Know. Glow Know **comes about from knowing that** glow **exists.** Adults would call this *awareness.* Glow **Amplification comes about from feeling good. Feeling good comes about from doing anything you love to do, or thinking anything you love to think, like** Glow Thoughts, **so you can make your** glow **stronger. When you do or think those things you feel good and you** glow **more.** I have translated these things into formulas.

"Shhh," Burst said, addressing the *cocuyo* lanterns, "The inner scientist speaks."

"I put together these formulas by studying myself and you guys. When we did certain things that we loved, like eat ice-cream, play sports, *VR Mind Voyage*, relax, Om Jam, or think Glow Thoughts, our glow **amplified** and EXPANDED.

"Glow Thoughts?" Burst looked puzzled.

"Glow Thoughts, for your information, are

positive thoughts that make you feel good," I said.

And, the opposite happens as well. When we stress out, feel lonely, angry or scared, our glow shrinks.

"You must be on to something big, 'cause your tree is bubbling again," Burst said, jumping up and popping bubbles in the air.

I continued. We can apply these formulas to reconnect with and **amplify** our glow. I have developed some basic ones to explain," I jiggled the test tubes in Voyager Pac to demonstrate. I used extreme caution, of course, to prevent another glow blast.

I gathered the *cocuyos* together to do their magic. Their bioluminescent taillights could write glow words that glowed in mid-air. I took out the test-tube and shook the contents to release a cloud of glow. The *cocuyos* whirled through the glow. They wrote these words which hung behind suspended in the air:

Glow Thoughts + Mind Travel =
Feeling Stellar and Glow Amplification

Flush It Out + Repetition of Glow Thoughts =
Glow Amplified

Glow Thoughts + Relaxation =
Glow Amplified

Glow Thoughts + Om Jammin =
Major Glow Amplification

"And if you use them all, you really have a Glow Blast," I added, "not that you want to do that."

Having highlighted all of this, I get that it is our mission to show other kids the power of glow. You know that deep-down all kids want to feel good, to feel the glow."

Burst did a double flip in that moment and landed on Luna's main branch inside the

WizDome. "Lums, you are brilliant! I totally get what you're trying to say. When I play sports, I get in the Zone. In the Zone, and after, I Glow Know and **amplify** my glow. So, is this the play where I get to pass the puck and share some glow?" I nodded but then his forehead wrinkled, and he frowned. "But, there are thousands, millions, billions, I don't know, totally a lot of kids around. How do you think we'll accomplish this mission impossible?"

"Stuart, dude, I'm thinking that there is no such thing as impossible when you are in touch with your glow," Shantanu said.

Voilà is a French expression for "there".

"All we gotta do is create some constellations of Glow Thoughts, and *voilà!!!*," I said.

Mission Possible

"OK I get ya'. By the way, check it out, your tree branches are lighting up," Burst said. Bubbles began to pour in through the windows, and the WizDome branches sparkled like crazy.

We all sat in silence for a moment, except for Burst who began to swing and catch bubbles while hanging upside down.

"Do you ever chill out?" I asked him as I pulled the Light Journal from my pack.

He grinned broadly and began to play air hockey UPSIDE-DOWN. I started to think out loud, holding my Light Journal for inspiration. Burst started reading a paper stuck to the back of the journal with iridescent dried goo, as I was reading the notes.

Sci ....ence Fig, no Fair Pro Ject?

"Shooting Stars! You are a genius Burst.

That is it!" The ideas began to fall on me like a hot, steaming radioactive meteor storm.

Quickly I unrolled a huge piece of drafting paper, Burst jumped down off the branch, and we all began to scribble at once. Somehow our minds connected in that moment to form the perfect neural net of communication.

A neural net is a cluster of brain cells, or neurons, that group together like a fishing net. The net catches thoughts like fish. The more you repeat a series of thoughts, (positive or negative), together, the more the neurons connect to form a net.

Melting rocks of Venus! As we finished, I jumped up. We had charted the plans at the exact moment of the nightly lunar spotlight on the WizDome. I opened the trap door to let the moon's celestial light in, and it lit up our paper. I used the pointer to highlight my cyclical diagram on the floor that read: Glow Thoughts **amplify** glow power (feelings of glow) which then produce more Glow Thoughts."

"The perpetual motion of glow. Right?"

Shantanu said, nodding.

I leapt to the table, brushing aside a star fruit tart with my foot. I was about to make an announcement, when Burst and Shantanu started laughing.

"What is it?" I asked.

"Dude, your socks are still a little galactically mixed up," Shantanu mused.

I rolled my eyes. "Don't you dudes get it? This is my new fashion statement. I have realized that my glow is not directly proportional to my matching socks, or any other part of my wardrobe for that matter. My socks don't **amplify** my glow. I am the one in charge of **amplifying** my glow, and I do through my thoughts and feelings. So, I decided that mismatched socks are cool for me. Thank you very much for noticing."

As I finished, I turned and noticed them staring at me wide-eyed.

"OK, cool with me." Shantanu said, and Burst nodded.

Then I made my announcement.

"Our first mission with Glow Know is to build a glow power generator. We will enter it in the science fair and introduce it to the whole Galileo Elementary!"

"So, it's like inner scientist gets in the Zone," Burst said.

"Uh, sure," I said. "Are you guys ready to blast forward?" I asked.

"I'm in," Burst said.

"I'm in," Shantanu said.

We then formed an agreement in writing and gathered around to sign. I was just about to sign my name when Burst interrupted.

"But, wait, Lums. We, like, don't build stuff very often. How are we going to put a generator together?" Burst worried.

I paused for a moment, then . . .a Glow Thought instead! "I know just the guy to do it. I will chat with him and then complete the agreement," I said.

"Groovy then," Shantanu said.

As we sealed the deal with a knuckle salute, bubbles started popping glow goo. Glow **amplified** to light up the WizDome even more.

Really Just The Beginning

So that brings me back to my room, here with Ori reading the Light Journal. He closed the book and glowed!

"And that is how the discovery of glow came about." I said. I was looking out of the window staring into space. That's when I realized that there wasn't an answer. I turned around.

My brother was glowing! He was lying on the floor, hunched over piles and piles of charts and diagrams. He was scribbling like a mad engineer, his sleeves were rolled up to his elbows and his forehead was scrunched like he was thinking intensely. The *cocuyos* were blinking all around him.

"Um, excuse me, Ori?" I said tapping him on the shoulder as I cleared my throat.

"Uh-huh," he mumbled and kept on drawing, folding papers into all sorts of designs.

Origami is the Japanese art of paper folding.

"Wouldn't want to interrupt your origami frenzy, but what exactly are you doing?" I asked.

"Lums, we have no time to waste, I figured you'd want some plans drawn up for the glow generator. So, I am drafting."

"You are so cosmically brilliant, Ori! I knew you'd get glowing once I let you in on the story. Here is our Master Agreement for the mission. I need you to sign, because this is top-secret sensitive information, and we can only share it after further scientific development," I said. I unrolled a scroll and placed it in front of Ori. I gestured where he should sign beneath Burst and Shantanu's signatures.

"Rare! Show me where. I've got work to do." Ori grabbed a compass and scribed his name, then turned back to the charts.

I felt the glow amplify around me as I picked up the pen. Then I signed my name and watched as our agreement began to glow.

That's when it hit me: The WizDome, with Luna as its gatekeeper, would be the meeting

Master Agreement

Mission Possible:
Glow Generator Construction

Goal:
Glow Re-connection
and **Amplification**

Luminas   Burst

Shantara   ORION

place for glow experiments. I stood up and announced to the moonflowers on the window: The WizDome from here on out is the glow meeting space. Kids from around the village will come here to learn about the wonder of glow. And from there on, we could even take glow from village to village to the entire world, creating our very own Glowmundo.

Meet the Authors

Jennifer Jazwierska

Jennifer has spent countless hours studying the difference between mind muck and glow thoughts. As a parent, storyteller, musician, and school psychologist, she has continually marveled and been inspired by the wisdom contained within the minds of children. As co-founder of Glowmundo, she resides in Colorado where she experiments daily with glow **amplification**.

Candice Bataille Popiel

Candice's childhood in Venezuela and her work in over 40 countries around the world, have prompted her to become an expert in the daily application of imagination travel. She sees the world as her playground and her life passion is the support of the development of human potentiality. She co-founded Glowmundo and is currently in Colorado glowrifically co-creating her life.

Meet the Artists

Thom Buchanan and **Jill Haller**, along with their daughter Ivy, love to create magical artwork of all kinds in their Colorado studio. They can be emailed at HallerBuchanan@hotmail.com

Information on Glowmundo
and opportunities for collaboration,
can be found by visiting

www.glowmundo.com

The **GLOWMUNDO** series is available at bookstores, on-line and at www.glowmundo.com

Each book of the Glowmundo series will focus upon an aspect of glow, providing self-awareness tools that support thinking beyond circumstances.

Be on the lookout for the release of the next book in the Glowmundo series.

Get ready to join me and my friends for more glowing adventures !